This Little Tiger book belongs to:

_____

_____

_____

For Dorcas
L.J.

For Mum and Dad
T.W.

LITTLE TIGER PRESS
An imprint of Magi Publications
1 The Coda Centre, 189 Munster Road,
London SW6 6AW
www.littletigerpress.com

First published in Great Britain 1995
by Little Tiger Press, London
This edition published 2010

tom's tail

Linda Jennings

Tim Warnes

LITTLE TIGER PRESS

Tom's tail was curly like a rolled-up rubber band.
It was a very neat little tail for a piglet,
but Tom thought it looked silly.

In all other ways Tom
was a proper little pig.

He was a nice pale pink with dirty patches where he
had wallowed in mud. He slurped and snuffled in the
pig trough with his brothers and sisters and made all
the usual piggy noises.

But how he wished he had a straight tail!

Sam the sheepdog
had a lovely, furry tail.

Henry the horse
had a long, swishy tail.

And Betsy the cow had
a thin, stringy tail with
a little tuft on the end.

"Even the rat's tail
is nicer than mine,"
said Tom sadly.

"Why don't you get your tail straightened?" said Henry.
"How?" asked Tom.
"Like this," said Henry as he put a big hoof on the end of Tom's tail.
"Now walk away."

Tom squealed and squeaked as he began to walk . . .

His tail stretched out and, when it had uncurled all the way, Henry lifted his hoof.

Ping!

Back sprang the tail . . .

and Tom hurtled
forward . . .

"OUCH!" yelled Tom and Sam together.

"I'll tell you what," said Sam, picking himself up.
"Why don't I take hold of your tail and you can
lead me along. That should straighten it out!"
So Tom took Sam for a walk, past the pigsty . . .

around the pond . . .

and over the buttercup field.
  "That's enough!" squealed
Tom. "Let me go!"

Ping!

Back sprang the tail to its
usual curly self. Tom felt sad.

Betsy looked at Tom,
and chewed thoughtfully.
Suddenly she had a very
good idea. She told Sam . . .

who took hold of Tom's tail again and stretched it.
Then he pushed the tail into a big patch of gooey,
sticky mud! He made Tom lie with his tail covered
in mud for a very long time, until . . .

the mud dried, and Tom's tail
was set into a long, thin pencil.
"Yippee!" cried Tom.

He twirled around, trying to see his new straight tail.

"OUCH!" said Sam. Tom's pointy tail had poked him in the chest.

"You look so silly," said Tom's mother.
But Tom liked looking different from the
other pigs.

"I'll wag my tail like Sam does," he said.
Whack! Tom's tail hit his sister in the face
and then poked his brother's behind.

"Stop it, Tom!" they both shouted.

When it was dark, Tom's mother gathered in all
her piglets for the night. They liked to snuggle up
in a big heap. But Tom's tail got in the way.

"Go away!" cried all Tom's brothers and sisters,
and they chased him right out of the pigsty.

Poor Tom! He tried to curl up outside but it wasn't very comfortable to lie down with a tail as stiff as a pencil. Finally, though, he was able to fall asleep.

During the night it began to rain, but Tom went on sleeping.

As it rained, the hard mud softened and slid off Tom's tail.

By the time morning came, his tail was as curly as it had ever been. Grunting happily, Tom went back to the pigsty.

"Who wants a straight tail anyway?"
said Tom later, as he pushed into the
trough with all his brothers and sisters.

"Now if I had a long, elegant nose like Henry the horse instead of this silly, stumpy snout, I could really get at that food!"

More fantastic reads from Little Tiger Press!

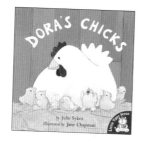
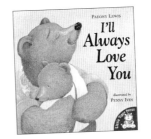

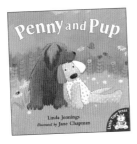

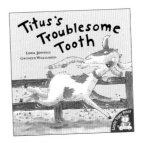

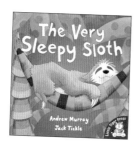

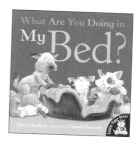

For information regarding any of the above titles or for our catalog, please contact us:
Little Tiger Press, 1 The Coda Centre, 189 Munster Road, London SW6 6AW, UK
Tel: +44 (0)20 7385 6333 • Fax: +44 (0)20 7385 7333 E-mail: info@littletiger.co.uk • www.littletigerpress.com